PUNISHED

L.V. Lane

Copyright © 2021 L.V. Lane

All rights reserved.

ISBN: 979-8-73636122-9

This is a work of fiction. Names, characters, businesses, places, events and incidents are either the products of the author's imagination or used in a fictitious manner. Any resemblance to actual persons, living or dead, or actual events is purely coincidental.

All rights reserved. This book or parts thereof may not be reproduced in any form, stored in any retrieval system, or transmitted in any form by any means—electronic, mechanical, photocopy, recording, or otherwise—without prior written permission of the author.

CONTENTS

Chapter One	Pg 1
Chapter Two	Pg 12
Chapter Three	Pg 24
Chapter Four	Pg 33
Chapter Five	Pg 41
Chapter Six	Pg 49
Chapter Seven	Pg 57
Chapter Eight	Pg 64
About the Author	Pg 71

CHAPTER ONE

Avery

As I sit at my desk, the words elude me again.

I don't need the money anymore. It's not been about that for a while.

But I just want to write about something other than *him*.

Outside the window, a storm is gathering. New England is always beautiful, but particularly during fall. My house, a three-story rambling creation of weatherboard, nestles among the trees. I love this view. But I love the worlds inside my head more.

I sigh.

I think about getting another coffee, although I don't think it will help.

Outside, the clouds darken, picking up in speed as they envelop the canopy of the trees. My sunglasses are sitting on the patio table, and my sweater is hanging over the back of the chair. I should go and fetch them in, yet all I do is stare at the looming clouds.

Am I lonely?

I don't think I am. I don't think I've been lonely a single day of my life, and whether or not someone was around.

No one is around today. The trauma when I discovered Peter was having an affair with a woman more steeped in reality than me no longer holds the potency it once did.

He didn't love her, he said. He was sorry, he said.

People drift in and out of love. I get that. I have seen that in other people.

And I have seen it in myself.

It still fucking hurt.

We tried again, but some breaks cannot be smoothed over or mended. We came to an understanding that involved Peter taking a job in another state.

I don't miss him. I even feel happy that he has now found someone else.

He sends me emails from time to time. I don't know why. My replies are functional. I give the appropriate response to pictures of his daughter, nearly a year old now. It's my own fault for my stupid, graceless blabbering as I drove him to the airport and suggested we remain friends.

I could put a stop to it. Tell Peter politely that I'd rather we both let this go. Tell him to fuck off with his pretty new wife who is so different from me. I have a destructive personality, according to my dear mother. And I continue to open the emails, although it only serves to rub salt into the wound.

Time has a way of bringing clarity. He was not for me, nor I for him. It's the lingering sense of failure that troubles me the most.

The first spots of rain tinkle as they hit the window.

It's morning, and I should be writing, but I can already sense today is a lost cause.

Pushing my chair back, I stand, leaving my pretty office with its white-washed walls and watercolors before taking the stairs two at a time. Sometimes meditating can help me to center myself.

I'm delusional; I know this. When one story is pulling to me, I need to submit. But I don't want to submit. Yesterday I allowed myself to write another chapter. One chapter turned into two, and before I knew it, I was writing about *him* again.

My bedroom is darkened with the turn in the weather. The peach and cornflower blue comforter is a little fussy for my taste, but it was a present from my mother, and the cotton quality is divine.

I don't bother to undress, just slip off my house shoes, and lay down on top. Hands crossed over my tummy, I give in and close my eyes.

Obsession, such an ugly word. Is it better or worse that the man in question isn't real?

I don't care anymore. I'm too far gone. Too invested. Too fucking lost.

A stream is gurgling to my left. I can't see it from here, for the forest is dense. Before me is a path, dappled in sunlight. The air is warm and heavy with the perfume of flowers. The forest is safe. This is my forest, after all. When you use your imagination to craft things, you have complete control to make them as pleasant or unpleasant as you desire. No committees, no third-party or enquiring friends. It's just me and my imagination.

At times I have been a magnanimous god, and I've also been a cruel and wicked master. No judgments exist here in this place except mine.

The forest path is narrow and soft under my feet. As I

look down, I realize that I'm still wearing my jeans and T-shirt. My feet are bare, for my feet were bare when I lay upon the bed. Sometimes I don't think about such details, but that doesn't matter, for I could never hurt myself in a dream.

I could make the path of any length, but I find that a walk allows me to sink deeper into the dreamscape. Soon it begins a steady descent, taking me down and down, ever steeper until I emerge into a valley. The fields before me are lush and green with fir trees lining the slopes to either side. In the very center of the valley is a magnificent multicolored tent.

The tent is my secret chamber.

It's the place where all possibilities exist.

It is the place where I can enter my dreams to a deeper, more profound level. Here, I'm connected to all things that I have known and all things that can be. Past, present, strangers, and people I hold dear. It is the place of my highest creativity.

The tent is an illusion, of course, as all things here are. Inside I can create worlds, or sometimes, like today, it is merely a tent. The silk of the flap is soft under my fingertips as I push it aside and enter. After the warmth outside, the tent is pleasantly cool. Brightly colored cushions line the floor. On the left is a wooden table bearing a bowl, a cloth, and a platter of fruit. A royal blue carpet is plush underfoot.

I let the flap fall behind me, creating a seal. Closing my eyes, I breathe deeply, drawing the clean scent into my lungs and letting it calm me. When I am here, I am at peace. There are no troubles to intrude, no people calling to see if I'm okay. There is no news of distant wars. The only things that may enter this chamber are things that I dictate.

Opening my eyes, I approach the table and, scooping up a handful of water, wash my face. Crushed petals float in the water. It leaves me refreshed. Picking up the towel, which is neatly folded to the side, I wipe my face and hands. The brightness outside keeps the tent well illuminated, although a couple of lamps have been lit and add a cheery glow.

When I am in my real home, I never feel alone, but here within the tent, and for the first time in a long while, I am strangely at odds.

I am waiting, I realize. I am waiting for *him* to arrive.

The sound of the tent flap opening behind me sets the hairs on the back of my neck prickling with awareness.

"Don't you have better things to do than taunt me by bringing me here?" His voice is smooth, cultured, and yet masculine.

I shiver. It is hard to remain unaffected given I designed it.

Steeling myself, I slowly turn.

It is impossible to be near Haden and not feel the impact of his presence. The things he has done are both monstrous and beautiful. Then there is his physical presence. He is tall, solid, and classic warrior to the bone. Wild, uncivilized, and deadly, he is all these things and more. When I first created his world, I wanted to make him the embodiment of its warrior class people. In his world, like in all worlds, there is diversity, but in any world, Haden is exceptional. Today, he is dressed for war, with black plate and leather armor. He is at ease in it and in himself.

At a glance, one might presume him to be a man. He is not a man; he is an alien.

"I missed you," I say before I can think better.

His grunt is derogatory. There is something different about him today. He feels more *real*, although that does not make any sense.

There is a little blood splattered on his armor, and I find myself staring at it.

The new story, the one I have begun writing, is never far from my thoughts. I left him in limbo at the end of the trilogy, doomed to forever be at war. He won't be happy if he realizes I'm writing once again.

"How can you possibly miss me?" he demands in that cool, clipped tone. His expression is impossible to read. His eyes, like his hair, are a golden brown. They have a mesmerizing quality with their oversized pupil and shifting iris color that moves like clouds. No woman would describe Haden as anything but handsome despite two noticeable scars on his face and in spite, or perhaps because of his ruthless reputation. "You created me, remember." He pauses to glance around the decadent tent before returning his sharp gaze to me. "Created me and then put me through hell before leaving me to wallow in eternal misery."

This is not a new conversation. I made him bitter and designed him to be blunt.

"It was not all misery," I say, recognizing the inflammatory nature of the words only as they leave my mouth.

His nostrils flare. A heartbeat later, he steps up to me and wraps a hand around my throat.

I gasp for air, shocked to my very core. He has never touched me before. Not once. At times I've convinced myself I've caught his scent or felt the air move as he passes.

But he has never once touched me.

The lack of air seems of secondary consideration to my catatonic state.

His hand is rough and warm, the power in it, terrifying. Today, I do not doubt that I can scent his rich, musky smell. I can see the flecks of darker and lighter brown in his impossible swirling eyes. I can see the individual hair follicles of his rough beard. This close, the jagged scars are more dreadful, yet he is still otherworldly in his beauty.

I am sinking. I don't fight the pull of unconsciousness.

If I die now, as improbable as it may be, I will find the peace I crave.

The pressure eases as swiftly as it arrives, although he does not lift his hand away. I gasp hoarse air into my lungs, dizzy, disorientated, and shaken.

His lips tug up in a smirk that makes me shiver.

When he smiles, I can see his fangs.

When he smiles, I remember that he is not a man but an alien, one I created in a book.

"Well, that was a surprise, wasn't it? Never expected I could touch you . . . Or choke you." Then his smirk fades, leaving cold and empty in its place. "Don't make allusions to her again, even in passing. Is that why you brought me here today, to fucking gloat?"

I shake my head. "No, I said I missed you, and I meant it." The book, the one I have recently started to write, is like a hammer in my skull.

His eyes shift over the tent. "It feels different today." He glances back down at me. "Is this part of the construct? Is this part of another story? Are you even fucking real?"

His frown deepens when I don't answer. I don't have an answer to give.

"Are you creating again, oh mighty creator? Are you weaving your evil games?"

"I—I don't know. This isn't a story. This is something

else."

His eyes narrow, and his thumb skims up the side of my throat in a sensual move. I try desperately to contain my reaction, but I swallow.

"Well, that was interesting, wasn't it?" He repeats the movement, rough thumb light against my skin. "You may be a twisted bitch, but your beauty is as undeniable as your satin-soft skin. Did you make me this way? Did you make me predisposed to find you a temptation encased in very real and very human flesh?"

"No," I say, shaking my head. "No, this was never part of it."

His thumb presses a little deeper into the pulse point. I find myself squirming and getting hot all at once.

Face lowering close to mine, so close I can feel his breath bathing my skin, he asks, "Are you creating again?"

A thud kicks off at the base of my throat as my pulse leaps under his thumb. My mouth opens, but words don't come out.

"Answer the fucking question!"

"Yes!"

He reels back, although he retains his hold on my throat. "Is this part of the story?"

My lips tremble and tears prick the back of my eyes. "No," I say quietly. "This is not part of the story."

He smirks again. The monster who roared his demands is tempered for the moment. "So this is outside."

"I think so. You're right. Something is different today. I don't know what has happened."

"But I can touch you," he says. "I can do anything I might do in the real world?"

I want to tell him that he doesn't have a real-world, that he is nothing but a piece of my imagination that I have written down into a book. But today, my understanding of reality is falling short. What is reality? What is this tent compared to the bedroom with the peach and cornflower blue chintz bedspread that my mother bought? The question of reality has baffled philosophers since man first emerged from the dirt. Who am I to presume to know?

I don't know a thing, and certainly not this alien who is like a stranger today and who still holds me by the throat.

Maybe I'm merely a piece in someone else's book?

This possibility rocks me.

His amber eyes darken further. It is subtle. Yet, I am so attuned to him with every fiber of my being that I know the moment his interest shifts from one state to the next.

CHAPTER TWO

Haden

Her throat feels delicate under my rough hand. She has to be sore after I nearly choked her out. But she doesn't let it show.

I hate her. I want to end her fucking life. I want to snap this pretty neck and watch the life leave her eyes. I've killed people before, lots of them. So many fucking people they are nothing but a blur. I'm not a good person. I'm a soldier. I'm a leader. I'm powerful, and I fucking love my power.

I loved something else once, but this bitch took it away.

I shouldn't want her. Yet I do, and I know this is another trick at play. I didn't know what this place was when she first started calling me here. It took many visits before I realized that she was my creator.

It wasn't her fault, she said. The characters take on a life of their own, she said.

Fucking bitch, I should snap her fucking neck and be done with it. Then maybe I'd sleep better at night.

Only I don't snap her neck, and my rage has gotten all twisted up with a rampant kind of lust.

Cruel lust.

"I want to kill you," I say. Sick bastard that I am, I enjoy the way tears pool in her eyes. "But there are worse things than dying."

She knows what I mean, what I am *inferring*. She made me, and I think she will enjoy whatever the fuck I do, so I'm going to need to be extra cruel. Almost choking her out didn't faze her. That's okay. I have an extensive repertoire of sadistic games, as she undoubtedly knows.

"It's been a long time since I had the pleasure of punishment-fucking a beautiful woman."

She shakes her head, big, pretty, blue eyes imploring me to show mercy.

"You know the way this is about to go, don't you, Avery Sinclair, god, and writer?" I sink my thumb into the soft flesh of her throat deep enough to challenge her airflow. "You've woven such a scene a time or two. Maybe I'll re-enact one of them. Or maybe I'll delight you with something new."

My time here is short. I sense that. The moment I let Avery leave, the moment the connection breaks, whatever power I have will be gone. Maybe someone else is writing this? Perhaps we are both caught up in another game by another god?

I don't care about what after. The bitch is writing again, making another story for me. Maybe she will be a kindly god, maybe she will show me love and happiness and an escape from the endless fucking war.

No, she's a bitch through and through. This is my time. I'm going to embrace every depraved fantasy she's built into my mind and play them back to her.

"Strip," I say, giving a little squeeze to her throat to make sure she understands this is not open to discussion.

The defiant fucking brat dares to shake her head.

"Strip, or it will be my pleasure to cut these clothes from you."

She doesn't strip. Not even when I release her throat. My grin is all teeth as I ease my knife from its sheath. Her stumbled step backward doesn't help her. I follow. I like this chasing. I hope she turns and tries to run.

Disappointment blooms when she trips on a pillow and falls into the soft, silken mountain at my feet.

"No!" She tries to ward me off, but it's pitiful.

"Tiny, weak little thing, what are you hoping to do?" I catch hold of her shoulder as I come down over her wriggling body, the blade glinting with all the menace I feel. "Hold very still, or I will cut you." I grin. Her eyes widen in a way that tells me she's looking at my fangs. "On second thoughts, struggle all you like."

She goes deathly still. I don't think she breathes. Her pretty eyes are wide and filled with terror.

"I'm going to be real honest here," I say, slipping the blade under the collar of her T-shirt and drawing it slowly down. The material disintegrates, falling apart in a delightful way. "Your fear is turning me on. I'd feel bad about it, but yeah, you didn't make me that way."

Her heaving tits make my mouth water as her former shirt pools to either side of her body. The bra that shields her from my view needs to go. I watch her face for a reaction, then slip the blade under the center where the two cups connect. It springs open to her sobbed gasp.

"Hush," I say. "I'm going to be getting very acquainted with all of you. This is only the first step." I run the back of the blade over her stiff nipple, bringing another stuttered sob bubbling from her lips. "These are pretty tits. Keep very still, Avery. I wouldn't want to cut this pretty, fat little nipple before I've had a taste."

Tears are spilling down her cheeks, and I wipe them away with the pad of my thumb. "You are so beautiful like this." I lean down to brush my lips over her dampened cheek. Tailing the tip of my tongue over the salty residue, I pull it into my mouth. "Fucking delicious," I say. "I bet your pussy is already wet. Shall we check?"

"I'm sorry," she says. "I'm sorry, okay. Is that what you want to hear?"

Leaning up, I take the blade to the material where it is caught over her arms. I am rougher than I might be as I finish slicing her T-shirt and bra away. She hisses as I draw a little blood.

"You're a fucking animal," she says, eyes spitting fire.

I only grin. Although I'm more careful about her pants. There is not a single nick to her creamy skin as I slice the remainder of her clothing away.

The little bitch curses me out the whole time, although she does stay very still. I could tell her to shut up. Gag her or threaten to slit her throat if she doesn't mind her words. But I find I enjoy her rebelliousness. It adds a little flavor.

"Open," I say, tapping the back of my blade against the top of her very naked little pussy slit. "Not a bit of hair. I like this very much." I'm riveted as she huffs out a token complaint before easing her thighs apart. "Keep very still."

I swear she doesn't breathe again as I scrape the back of the blade over the plump, glistening folds. I reverse the blade as I near the little clenching treasure in the center . . . And sink the handle slowly in.

I watch her face as I fuck the handle in and out. Waiting for that moment when it squelches. Her face twists and colors an enticing shade of red. "You destroyed everything and everyone I ever cared about. You're very fucking wet for a woman about to be punishment-fucked by a ruthless killer holding a grudge."

Her pretty eyes plead with me.

Yeah, that's not going to work out well for her.

"You feel tight, Avery. I think it's going to be a challenge when I force my cock deep in here. I think there might be a bit of pain. But that can't be helped. It is a punishment-fuck, after all."

I sink the handle all the way in. "Clench for me," I say, watching the blade bob. "Good girl. Now hold it there for me while I get undressed." I stand up, watching her fight her instinctive desire to push it out. It has a bit of weight. I'm sure it's an alarming situation knowing it could cut her badly should it fall.

She sobs and pants. Her pussy is very slick around the handle. There is a real danger it could slip.

"Grip the fucking handle," I say as I strip from my clothes. Tossing everything aside without a care for where or how it falls. Her eyes are on me the whole time, chest stuttering even as her gaze roams over what I expose. If her feverish expression is anything to go by, she likes what she sees. As my pants drop and I fist my cock, the little bitch swallows.

Obsession. Perhaps I'm not the only one suffering from this affliction.

Then my eyes drop to the bobbing, lethal blade handle wedged inside her hot little cunt.

"I can't," she sobs. "Please, I can't."

I don't think she is faking it, and the handle is fucking slick.

The dam breaks on her tears as I take it out and toss it aside. I like her fucking tears. They make me as hard as the sight of her drenched pussy does. Taking her hips in hand, I line up and thrust deep. Her scream says it hurts a lot. I admit, she's a fucking insane level of tight. I don't let any of this stop me. I pound the fuck out of her, take a better hold, and fuck her deeper still.

I'm bottoming out, but that doesn't stop me either. This is a punishment, and I fucking hate everything about her except this wet, filthy, gripping cunt.

I see the moment it stops hurting. She goes fucking wild, bucking, screeching, raking me with her nails even as her pussy creams all over my cock. I try to fuck her harder. I don't want the bitch to enjoy it. I don't want her to fucking come.

But she does.

The tiny, fragile, beautiful woman who has subjected me and everyone I loved to immeasurable cruelty moans with wild abandon as she comes all over my cock.

I am momentarily stunned. There is no other term I can find to describe the seizure that takes hold of my chest. The sense of closeness disgusts me. I want her to suffer like she made me suffer.

Her guttural cry as I pull out barely tempers my rising aggression. I flip her onto her front where I don't need to look at her pretty blue eyes begging me to find restraint.

My cock is hard enough to break rocks. I want to ram it in her ass. I *want* her to hurt.

"You ever been ass fucked?" I say, spearing a finger into that tightly puckered hole. It's super slippery after she has come, and my finger slides in and out easily despite the tightness. "Well, this is fucking tight."

"Go to hell!" She struggles, but it's weak and barely troubles me.

I smirk. The fire is back. I can admit I like the fire. "I'm guessing that's a no." I pump my finger in and out. She is already fluttering around me even as she's trying to wriggle away. I force another finger in.

"Haden, please. I can't. You can't. It will tear me."

It's the first time she has ever used my name, and it brings an unexpected steadying influence on the red haze filling my mind. "Ah, baby, bet you wish you didn't write me a ten-inch dick now. It's going to be a squeeze. But I do enjoy a challenge. As you would know."

I feel calmer now I can no longer see her face.

I don't only want to hurt her.

I find I want her to feel pleasure, after all.

I want to ruin her fucking life just like she ruined mine . . . Like she's about to ruin it once again given she has started another book.

But I want to ruin her in ways that the eyes do not see.

I want to ruin her for all other men. I want her to think about me. I want her to obsess about me the way I've come to obsess about her.

"It won't tear," I say. "Not if I'm careful and stretch you first. Isn't that how this works? Oh yeah, my bad. Clearly, you don't have a fucking clue how this works given you've never had this cherry popped. That was a rookie mistake, surely, writing about something you've never done?"

She's wriggling, but her heart isn't in it. If her twitching and half-smothered moans are anything to go by, she's taking to her first ass reaming well.

"I've never written it!" she sobs.

I stop, fingers still speared in her ass. "You haven't?"

"No, I fucking haven't!"

I've done this before many times. I like ass fucking, especially for a punishment-fuck, which this still is. How can she not have written it?

"Brace yourself," I say. That is all the warning she gets. My fingers ease out, and my cock takes their place. "Fuck, you are tight," I grunt as the tip breaches the puckered entrance. "Stop fucking clenching."

She doesn't. But I'm in now, and I'm committed to deep fucking this ass.

"Fucking heaven," I say as I begin to thrust slowly in and out. She is nice and slippery after her climax, and my cock penetrates easily despite her fierce clenching. Tightening my grip on her hips, I begin to fuck her deep and hard. Her wails are sharp and visceral. But I'm fucking determined, and her ass has no choice but to give.

Then it does, and her new wails bring a tightening to my balls and an urgency to my thrusts.

"Good girl. All opened for a nice, deep, ass reaming." My words make her clench, and no sooner does she clench than those sweet contractions start, and she comes with garbled, panted, moans. I grit my teeth against the pull, but I can't hold back. My hips slam and jerk against her as I empty load after load of hot cum into her ass.

When I come down from the high, I realize she's sobbing again. This despite her tight ass continuing to clench over my cock. There is no easy way to do this. I am deep inside her. The pulling out is normally pleasurable, but I think she's sore, and it's going to sting like a motherfucker.

I pull out. A great gush of frothy cum pours out. It's both grim and deeply satisfying at the same time.

"Oh! Fuck! You are a fucking savage!"

I bite back a chuckle. For a god and creator, she has a filthy mouth.

Then I sigh as she tucks into a ball and presses her hand over her bottom like that might help. "You wrote me to be a savage. You shouldn't be surprised when I act like one." When I started this, I wanted to make her bleed. But now I'm only relieved that there is no serious damage where I have fucked her ass.

"Clearly, I didn't write all of you!"

She is right. Clearly, she didn't write all of me since she has never written about this. But then who did?

I flop down on the cushions beside her and stare at the tent ceiling. Her sobs are enough to soften me toward her. I pull her, despite strong and vocal protests, against me. "I'm not going to let fucking go, so you may as well get used to it."

"It fucking hurts!"

I huff out a breath. "Unless I am much mistaken, it was

not all pain."

Her tears peter out. She doesn't argue, so there is that. I want to tell her it won't hurt so much next time. But what is next time? I don't even know what the fuck this time is.

I've been lonely for so very long. Angry for longer. The soft, well fucked woman who is tucked in my arms might be a god and a creator of worlds, but she is not a monster. She cries, and she feels pain.

She feels unexpectedly like the most real thing I've encountered in my whole monstrous fucked-up life.

"I'm sorry," she says, so softly that I almost don't hear. "You were just words on a piece of paper . . . Well, on a computer, but you know what I mean."

I know of computers, for the world she created had those with technology and those without. I began in one part of the world and ended in another. I am a warrior now, more comfortable with a sword than a computer.

"I'm so sorry," she says again.

I sense her genuineness. I can neither dispute nor discount its realness in this unreal place. Is that all I am? A word on a piece of paper. If she stops writing and thinking of me, will I cease to exist?

Outside the tent, the sun is setting, and shadows fill the space.

CHAPTER THREE

Avery

I wake up in my bed. It is morning, but I don't think it is the same morning as when I lay down to rest.

As I shift, I wince. Either I've done crazy things to my ass with my vibrator while I slept, or it was far more than a dream. I'm still in my clothes, the ones Haden cut from my body, although they are now entirely whole. But as I sit, I feel the wet, slipperiness between my legs that speaks of what transpired.

"I'm going insane," I mutter, wincing and whimpering as I rise from the bed.

I sway a little as I gain my feet before padding into my adjoining bathroom. I don't want to pull my pants and panties down. I don't want to see it.

I don't want it to be real.

A cold sweat pops out along my brow as I find the evidence there in all its filthy glory.

I sit on the toilet. I go. It fucking stings, and all the cum splatters out in a way that makes more sweat pop out along my brow.

When I'm done, I strip, step into the hot shower and wash myself.

It's only after I'm done, as I am drying my trembling body on a fluffy towel, that I wonder if I've been the subject of a bizarre home invasion, and further, that I've been drugged.

I'm sick.

There is nothing in my stomach, but I still heave for a good long while before I can get it under control.

Wrapping myself up in my bathrobe, I do the sensible thing and pull up my home security footage on my computer. My hands shake as I work the mouse. It is all here—all of it. Only I'm quite alone as I writhe on the bed, hips rolling and mouth open as I scream my pleasure.

I snap my laptop closed.

It wasn't a dream. Dreams do not fill you with cum. Dreams do not make your ass feel like it has been breached by a watermelon.

"Ah, baby," he said. *"Bet you wish you didn't write me a ten-inch dick now. It's going to be a squeeze. But I do enjoy a challenge. As you would know."*

It felt real. And I think I must be going crazy because it couldn't possibly be so. If I close my eyes, I can feel his body against mine. If I breathe deeply, I'm sure his scent still lingers in my lungs. My stomach does that falling thing. No, I didn't make up the part where he stuffed me full of cum.

Making sense of this is impossible, so I don't try. I go downstairs and make myself a cup of tea because that's what people do when they've suffered a great trauma. Outside the window, I can see my sunglasses on the patio table. My sodden sweater hangs limply over the back of the chair. With a sigh, I take a packet of cookies from the pantry. Ripping it open, I bite a chunk of the cookie and all but inhale the sugar. It feels good as it hits my stomach. A half-eaten cookie in my mouth and a cup of tea in my hand, I return to my office.

I should put on some clothes. I should call my mother or a friend. I should research a good psychologist. But I don't feel like doing any of those things. Instead, I put my cup down on the pink cartoon cat coaster, and rest my cookie stash on top. Flipping open the lid on my laptop, I draw out my chair and get ready to write.

My ass is still sore, so I don't stay there long before I need to go and get a cushion.

Between the cushion, the cookie, and the tea, I find a form of comfort.

I lose myself in the words and the world. It's *his* world that I'm writing because this feels like the only way to make sense of what transpired.

When I'm writing, I don't need to look closely at the madness consuming my life. I don't need to acknowledge that I've gone crazy. Nor do I need to acknowledge that there's an alien's cum still leaking from my ass.

He calls me a god, but I'm not a god; I'm only a writer.

So I write. And the writing is cathartic. I forget all about the soreness engulfing my body. I forget about my half-drunk tea and the cookie crumbs on my desk. Not that it matters when I've either lost my mind or done the impossible and stepped outside of space and time.

It's dark when I rouse myself from my frenzy. I think this is the most I've written in a very long time. My body is stiff and sore in ways more than from my writing. My cup of tea has long gone cold. Even the cookie crumbs have been scattered. Pushing the laptop shut, I rise and make my way into the bedroom. I stare at my big, empty bed with the peach and cornflower blue comforter. Sleeping will bring the nightmare back.

Okay, I don't think it was all a nightmare. I think a lot of it was very pleasurable.

Savage. I called him a savage because that is what he is. That is what he has always been. And he was right; I made him so.

In a warped kind of way, I can understand his anger. In the interest of a story, I have done terrible things to him and those he loved. I broke him, again and again.

On my laptop is another story, one only partly written. Will this make it better? Or am I making a bigger mess?

I take another shower, drying myself off under automation before slipping on my nightgown and heading for my bed. I don't want to sleep. I *dare* not sleep. But I'm battered inside and out. I'm mentally and physically exhausted, and it pulls me under with ease.

The next day I find life to be entirely normal. There were no savage dreams last night lifting me to carnal highs. There is only my empty house, my computer, and the words that spill over and over onto the pages of my book. A week passes. I question my sanity. Did I make it all up?

I've lived an isolated life since Peter left. When was the last time I went out and met with friends? I can't remember it's been so long. So I decide to do precisely that. I call my friend, Helen, and we arranged to go out for a drink.

I take extra care with my makeup—some of it hasn't

been used in a year. I do my hair, and I put on a pretty dress. I'm about to strap on sandals that I've dug out from the back of my closet when the doorbell rings.

I'm expecting an Uber even if they are a little early. But when I open the door, it's not an Uber driver standing there.

It's *him*. How can it possibly be him? I stand gaping. It's a ridiculous reaction. But who wouldn't freak out if a character from a book turned up at their door? He's not dressed as a warrior today. He is wearing jeans and a T-shirt.

A very snug T-shirt.

A T-shirt that fits all the dips and ridges that make up his amazing body.

"You," I say inadequately. "Look a lot bigger in the flesh."

My eyes lower to his boots. He has really big boots. He is all very proportional, I realize with a blush.

When I can drag my eyes from his boots, I find him watching me. Brow raising, his lips tug up in a smirk that shows the tips of his fangs. Reminding me, as if I could forget, that he is an alien and not a man. His smile is at odds with our last encounter. It's the kind of smile I'd imagined him making but have never witnessed personally before. That smile stops and starts my heart. It makes me forget everything and everyone else.

My tummy turns over because he's directing it at me.

Obsession. I have long known that I've suffered from an obsession and that this alien male has been at the center of it all. I thought I knew everything about him. I created him, after all.

Or did I?

And I don't know everything about him, as he pointed out last time we met.

Taking hold of my shoulders, he walks me backward into my home. I don't think I blink as he turns and pushes the door shut. "What are you doing?" I ask like there might be a sensible answer to this. "How did you get here?"

"What am I doing? I believe I just entered your dwelling. How am I here? Well, I started off imagining the tent, but that didn't prove very helpful." He takes a strand of my hair between his fingers and thumb. I swallow and try to decide whether I should snatch it back. But he drops it and steps back before I can decide. "So I put one of these long ebony hairs that came back with me into the intergalactic database and opened up a wormhole."

My jaw is hanging slack. I shut it with a snap.

I didn't write wormholes and intergalactic databases into his world. But as I'm discovering, I didn't write a lot of things that have happened in his life. Space, time, and my understanding of reality bends and contracts. Was the tent merely at alternate reality or universe? Have I been opening up a wormhole every time I imagined being there?

How did my clothes return with me whole?

And how does any of this explain my control of his life?

My head hurts. I rub my temples as I take in the freakishly big alien in my hall. The context of him being here in my house, and not my sacred chamber, brings our great size disparity into stark relief. "You don't fit in my home," I say.

"I don't fit in a lot of places," he says, eyes turning hooded. "But that hasn't stopped me yet."

I swallow. It's like a great chasm opening up between us. His face softens. I don't think he's all bad. Certainly, I didn't make him all bad. Not the things that happened in his life, and not the things he did to me, either.

"How are you feeling?" he asks.

"Now?" I'm having trouble keeping up with this conversation. "Now I'm doing okay. If you'd asked me that question a week ago, I'd have gone with a train wreck."

"Yeah," he says. "I admit I was pissed."

"Are you still?"

"Some," he says. "Yeah, I've still got some rage to work through."

Why does my pussy clench at the thought of him working through his rage? I don't think I can survive that again, even though some parts of it were sublime. "I can't do it again."

"I'm not asking you to," he says.

"Then what are you asking?" I say. "Why are you here?"

"I'm here because I need to be." His eyes skim over my home as though familiarizing himself with it. "I'm here because I want to be." His dark, endless eyes that shift like clouds, and that have suffered too much pain settle on me. "I'm here because we have unfinished business."

CHAPTER FOUR

Haden

She is looking at me with a lot of fear and a little hope. I wish it were the other way around. But that's all on me.

I spent some time exploring this world before I arrived at her home. I can see that it's just another universe, full of ordinary people. It's a world where she is, in fact, a writer, just as there are writers in my world. And I don't know how this works or how she gained control over my life. But she did. And now I want to try and gain power for myself.

I don't know where my obsession with her first began, but it's well-integrated now. She must have called me to that tent a thousand times. In our early meetings, it held only a vague dream-like quality. But I noticed it became more and more real over time until the day when I finally touched her.

Then everything changed.

The doorbell rings behind me. My eyes narrow on Avery before I turn and snatch open the door. Who the fuck is here?

There is a human male on the other side. I must be projecting some of that rage I mentioned because he takes a hasty step back. "Someone ordered an Uber," he says.

Uber? What the fuck is an Uber?

I'm about to tell him to fuck off when Avery squeezes between us. "Sorry, I need to cancel," she says. "Please debit the cost from my account."

The man beats a hasty retreat. A small square card is attached to his vehicle window with the word 'UBER' on it, and a smaller tag line that I can't read from here.

She shuts the door while I'm still glaring at the vehicle and the human male who dared to interrupt us.

"I was going out," she says. Picking up a device from a narrow hall table, she begins tapping something onto it.

Maybe she's calling the local law enforcement? It will not

end well if she does.

The device dings. She taps something else onto the screen before putting it facedown on the table with a sigh.

"Do you have a lover?" I ask more casually than I feel. I don't see any evidence of another invested party in my not very subtle scoping, but I might be wrong.

"I—no, I had a partner a few years ago, but it didn't work out. It was me, not him."

A disparaging snort escapes me. If my life is any indication, Avery writes some pretty fucked up prose. "You're damn right it was you and not him," I say.

The fire is back in her eyes. "What the fuck would you know about me?"

I raise a brow. "I know fucking everything. All the dark crevices and filthy things that fill your mind since you wrote them into my life."

Heat fills her cheeks as she gives me a shifty look. "You have a point."

That sounds a lot like a concession. It sounds a lot like the end of the war and the beginning of negotiations.

"Take me to the room where you write," I say.

She gives me a look that I can't decipher. This is all fucking crazy, so maybe she thinks she's going nuts. I don't claim to understand, either. I'm just working with whatever the fuck my instinct tells me.

With a little puff of breath, she nods, and turning, says, "This way."

Her house is tasteful. My mother would like it here . . . My father not so much. My mother comes from the civilized part of my world. My father is a savage, like me. I grin to myself. Yeah, he's probably worse than me.

I feel my hairs stand to attention as we enter her creating room. Her *god* room. There are whitewashed walls with watercolors depicting sailboats and quaint fishing villages. Centering the window is a desk with a comfortable-looking chair. The wide window offers views across a forest. It's a lovely room with lots of light.

There, in the center of the desk, is a sleek silver laptop. Instinctively I know it's on here that she writes the words and where she conjures the adventures and misadventures of my life. It's a strange feeling looking at the machine. "So this is where it happens," I say. Keeping her face down, she nods.

"Okay, time to get down to it," I say.

Her head lifts, and her eyes search mine. She's not comfortable looking at me, but I guess she designed me to represent a hero, weird as that may be. I get the impression that she's much enamored with all facets of me, including my darkness and my more bloodthirsty side. I'm a big male, a warrior. I'm not stupid, and I've been told often enough that I'm pleasing to the eye. She's had complete control over me for so long, so it feels good to claw a little of that control back. And fuck it, I'm gonna fucking milk it.

I gesture towards the chair. "Take a seat," I say.

She pulls out the chair while eyeballing me like I'm about to pounce. It's only then that I notice the cushion. I look from her to the cushion and back again. The little brat rolls her eyes and removes the cushion with a huff. "You're a fucking savage, and I was fucking sore afterward."

My lips tug up in a smirk despite this being no laughing matter. "Ah baby, I'm sorry."

"Don't fucking baby me," she growls.

For a godly bitch, she sure likes to curse a male out. There's a satisfying gasp of outrage as I scoop her up. Taking a seat on the chair, I put her on my lap facing the desk.

The chair creaks a bit, but it holds.

She winces. "Are you still sore?" I ask.

"No!"

"Are you sure? Have you been to a medical person?"

She's a wriggling bundle of indignation on my lap, but I take a firm hold, and she's going nowhere.

"No! I haven't been to see a doctor. How's that going to work? I was ass fucked by an alien character from a book? They would lock me up!"

I bristle at the sharpness in her tone, but I can't really

blame her. "Your language is truly appalling. Maybe I should check you now?"

"You are not checking me! What do you even mean by check me? Like, check me by inserting your ten-inch dick?"

I laugh. I don't mean to laugh. But really, she's a test to anybody trying to keep a straight face when she says things like that. "You know I'm thinking about inserting my dick now. Rest assured, it won't hurt as much this time."

"How can you be amused by this?"

"I'm amused by your overreaction . . . And by your choice of words. I can see you found your calling when you became a fucking writer."

"You weren't here the next day, so how the hell would you know whether I'm overreacting or not?"

Way to make me feel like a prize chump. I probably deserved that. "Okay, let's call a truce. I didn't come here to discuss inserting my dick in your ass. As long as you're okay now, we can move on."

She nods. I take that as a yes.

"Open the laptop."

"Why?" There is suspicion in her tone.

"Because I want to see what you've written. And if I don't like it, I'm going to change it."

She twists to look back at me over her shoulder. "You can't change your life story. You can't dictate your own life."

"Who says? I've never much cared for what I can and can't do. Either way, I'm going to try."

She doesn't argue with me, and leaning forward, lifts the lid of the laptop. There's no lock screen. It's open on some sort of application.

My hands tighten around her waist. I feel a little cold and clammy as I realize what is written there. It's my name next to some quotes for some words that I'm supposed to say. I can't actually read the words. It's like they've gone completely blank in my mind. I try to read them; I really do. But all I can see is that one word, *my* word, my name, in a story.

It's unnerving. Not in the way of a battle and the rush and roar of conflict. But a deeper, more profound level of unease. It's not like I was confused about the fact that she was my creator. I've seen her hundreds of times in that tent. We've talked about—argued about it for most of them.

Yet seeing my name on that page, fuck, I have no idea what to feel.

Her body is trembling against mine. She's waiting for my reaction . . . For me to say how I feel.

My life tilts before my eyes. I'm hanging on the brink of falling, but somehow, I never do.

"Scroll back to the beginning," I say.

She does as she's told before trying to hop down. I tighten my hands on her waist. "Where the fuck do you think you're going?"

"I should leave you to it," she says.

"No, I like you here. We are going to read this together."

And we do.

So many words, elegant words, short words, long words, they merge together, creating a story that represents the next chapter of my life.

And I can see what she's doing. The direction the story goes is not an unpleasant one. It's exciting, as all my life was before I lost everything.

Yet this is not the life I would choose to write for myself. I read it all without judgment. She is quiet as I scroll through the pages. There are parts where she fidgets when the story grows tense. There are some challenges for me to yet endure. I don't mind the challenges, but I want a different conclusion from the one that she is drawing towards.

I want an ending with her in it.

And she is going to write it for me.

CHAPTER FIVE

Avery

"I want you to introduce a new character," he says. I'm still sitting on his lap. I've been sitting here all day. I don't claim it to be a comfortable thing. But it's not uncomfortable either. If I'm honest with myself, I quite like sitting on his lap and the strange tingly awareness growing between us.

"What sort of character?" I glance back at him over my shoulder, but he's giving me an indecipherable look.

Then his lips tug up on one side, showing a fang, and he says. "I want you to introduce yourself."

I try to get down. He's having none of it. I realized he was going to change the story to his liking. Maybe try to write back the person that he lost . . . the person I'm not allowed to talk about.

I don't think it would be possible, but I expected him to try.

But I didn't expect him to write me in. "How can I introduce myself? How can I write myself into my own story?" I ask.

He shrugs. "No idea, but I have faith in my creator. We'll start this chapter with you describing yourself."

His hands shift on my waist, one giant hand slides so that it is pressed over my tummy. "Or, if you don't fancy writing, I could check your ass for damage and try inserting my dick again."

If he was looking for a predictable reaction, I'm pretty sure he got it. He only laughs, amused at my expense as I splutter my outrage. I feel him lean back, settling into the seat. "Better start writing, baby."

I do because I sense this is not open to negotiation. And I'd rather do anything than go through *that* again.

Long ebony hair, blue eyes, five-five with too much ass...I pause because 'too much ass' is not going to cut it.

He growls. Leaning forward, he pulls the keyboard to the front of the desk and begins deleting and tapping new words.

I stare at his hands. Those huge, scarred hands that he was probably thinking about killing me with when he first put them on me a week ago. It's not until he sits back that I remember to look at what he wrote.

. . . an ass I want to sink my fangs into and tits that make me drool. . .

"That's not me," I say, scoffing and getting hot all at once. When I turn back, I see him smirking.

"It's how I see you."

"It's how I'm going to see you," he amends, eyes turning hooded like he's thinking about me naked. "I think I've earned the right to some input given all the shit you've put me through."

And just like that, all the humor is gone.

I feel bereft in a way Peter leaving me never caused. I feel lonely, although I rarely do.

He stands and deposits me on the chair on my own. It feels odd and uncomfortable after sitting on his lap for many hours while we read the story. He begins pacing the small room. He's so freaking big, and it unnerves me.

Then he leaves the room, and I breathe all the air that was missing into my lungs.

Has he gone?

This weird pressure is a strain, yet I can't bear the thought of him leaving and possibly never seeing him again. I know things have changed, that we have crossed lines that are not supposed to be crossed, maybe broken rules sacred to the universe.

But I don't want him to fucking go.

I hear a heavy thud and my heart races, wondering if it was the front door. But there is another thud closer, and then another.

He appears at my office door with an easy chair in his arms. It used to belong to my grandmother, and it's a beast of a chair. It took two removal guys to carry it into the house. "What on earth—"

It takes him three goes and some twisting of the chair before he can get it through the gap. "It's the only fucking chair that doesn't look like it will snap if I sit on it," he grunts, finally forcing it through and dumping it on the floor with a thud. "Fuck me, this chair is wild."

"It was my grandmother's," I say, trying and failing to keep the grin off my face. I remind myself that he's a dangerous predator, and I shouldn't be happy that he's still here.

"Well, I guess they built the furniture sturdy back in your grandmother's day." He disappears out of the room again, and I watch him leave with a frown.

He returns with a pack of beers . . . Like a whole pack. It must have been in the back of the fridge for six months or more. "I think that might have expired."

"Expired?" he asks, frowning at the beer. "I thought beer lasted forever?" Sitting down, he pops the lid off one and takes a hefty slug before examining the label on the bottle. "Given I'm a character in a book, I'm not sure I need to worry myself with things like produce dates. But it tastes fine, and we'll be here for a while." He tips the bottle in my direction. "Do you want one?"

I shake my head slowly. He's not *only* a character in a book. He's an alien who put a strand of my hair in an intergalactic database and traveled through a wormhole.

An alien who has gotten himself comfortable on Granny Mable's chair with enough beer for a party.

"Turn around," he says softly. "Fingers on the keyboard, and write what I tell you."

I do, and he does.

The words pour out of him, into me, and through my fingers onto the pages of the book. I write until the sun sets, and he puts the light on. I write into the night until my fingers cramp, and I can barely see the blurred words before me. The words merge and overlap in my mind. Orders, details, intricacies, and layers that enrich the world.

Sometimes he sits as he dictates, and sometimes he stands and paces the confines of my small room. I've no idea whether any of what he speaks will come to fruition. Maybe we are further breaking the laws of creation by what we try to do. I admit the story he weaves is exciting. I should love to join that world, and to be part of those adventures. For so long, I have been a millpond. But before me on the pages is a wild stormy sea with thrashing waves and excitement that makes my heart thud in my chest.

I think I zone out at times, lost in the process of tapping the words such that I don't notice what he says.

He is speaking now, and my fingers are flying even as I am arrested by what he says.

". . . He only has to look at me, and I feel my body respond. It doesn't matter how roughly he fucks me. I still come for him. And when he says those words 'Come for your master', I do."

I stop typing and throw a look at him.

I can feel my body responding like the determination is already cast in stone.

"You can't write that," I say.

His lips tug up before he lifts a bottle—it must be the tenth—and takes a slug. "I believe I just did. Shall we test if it works?"

"No!"

He nods his head at the laptop, and I turn back to my task. "And then there are times when he shares me with his friends."

My fingers stop halfway through the sentence. I feel cold and clammy. I feel like I might be sick. I wonder if exhaustion has caught up and my fingers have finally seized. I hit backspace until the whole sentence is gone.

I feel better instantly.

"Let's try that again," he says.

But my fingers don't move. They can't move. And further, I don't want them to.

He chuckles, and I hear the sound of a fresh beer being opened. "There we go. Looks like we have found a hard limit. Start typing again . . . I love to suck his cock. The feeling of it forcing deep into my throat, so deep that I can't breathe, makes my pussy absolutely drenched."

God help me; I write the words. I don't want to, yet I also want to, and they all go down onto the page. It's like the opening of a flood gate, and he tells me in that clear, clipped tone all the filthy things he's going to do to me. And other than that hard limit, as he calls it, I don't balk at a single one.

I can't feel my fingers by the time it draws to a close. The words are a jumble, and I merely a conduit for Haden's will.

I am roused from this stupor as I see *The End*.

Blinking slowly, I realize I've blanked out much of the book.

I try to scroll up, but a large hand enters from my left, and the laptop is snapped shut.

"I think I missed a bit of what was written," I say.

"I think you missed a lot," he counters. "But rest assured, your fingers stopped typing whenever they reached something you didn't like."

I want to take comfort in this, but I know many things made me squirm even as I wrote them.

Vows. *Binding* vows. The exact words slip through my mental fingers, but I know my body and life belonged to him by the end of the story.

"What happens now?" I ask. "Now that I've reached the end?"

CHAPTER SIX

Haden

I had a plan for today. One that did not involve fucking Avery, although I had hopes along those lines. There were things I missed out on last time. Things I want to do to her.

There are also things I did last time that I probably shouldn't have. Although I admit they were fucking hot at the time.

When I woke up alone in my bed after I fucked her in the tent, my first thoughts were ones of regret. A week earlier, and I'd have regretted not killing her while I had the chance. But after I'd touched her, I found my perspective had changed.

She was no longer a cold god weaving my fate. She was a real person with hopes, fears, and feelings.

I questioned myself.

I questioned reality and fantasy.

I questioned every event of note that had happened within my life.

I hoped she would call me to the tent again. I expected she would not.

My obsession with her began long ago. A dark specter who called me into her dreams and lorded over all the terrible things she had wrecked upon my life. Only she didn't lord, not really. It just felt that way at the time.

I'm still obsessed. I still want to hold domination over her life the way she once held mastery over mine. But now it is the control and power of a lover and not a broken man hungering for her death.

That her fingers only balked at a few of my suggestions tells me she is averse to none of this.

I think she might even need this, for I now understand the extent and weight of her guilt.

It is a burden and one I will free her of.

"What will happen now?" she asks again, voice no more than a whisper.

"Now I take you to bed, and I show you that I'm not all savage," I say.

Those soulful blue eyes stare up at me without focus. I gather up Avery's small hands and massage them gently. She has done an unnatural amount of writing today. It was like we were both caught under a spell.

"That feels nice," she says.

I have a strange notion that this forthright god who held power over me and my life is feeling shy.

I pick her up and carry her, with some trial and error, to her bedroom. It's a nice space with the same whitewashed walls. The pictures here are larger and more impressionist in style. The bed is a dark wood creation with a thick comforter in pastel shades. Low lights come on when I tap the switch on the wall.

I wonder what she will think of my home when she sees it . . . What she will think of my bed. But then I remember that she knows it as well as she knows me, given she wrote such details within her books.

If she sees it, I amend. I still don't have a fucking clue if any of this will work. Wormholes use quantum physics, and they are anything but exact. Sometimes things can get lost or distorted in the transition from one place to the next.

And yeah, sometimes the things getting lost or distorted are sentient beings.

Tomorrow is an unknown. Tomorrow has ever been an

unknown for me, but with her writing, it might just change. I don't think she understood most of what I told her to write. She zoned out for much of it. But it wasn't the future, per se. It was the backstory for a new character who is about to enter my life.

Who wants to live a life already mapped out? I don't. I want to write my own story, but I want to write it as I go. I want the book open and full of possibilities.

There is a stammered protest as she makes contact with the bed. I think she is going to push me away—I wouldn't blame her. But instead, she leans up and presses her lips to mine.

I groan into her mouth as I press her back into the bed. That first tentative touch is like igniting a flame, and we both burn hot. Fist in her hair, I open my mouth over hers. The little needy whimper I swallow finds a direct line to my balls. I want to fucking consume her. I want to do absolutely filthy things to her. I want her screaming as she comes all over my cock. Open, giving, and available for my pleasure. I have so much pleasure I want to take. But this time, I also want to give.

So, yeah, I had a plan for today. One that did not involve fucking Avery. But now that I'm here in her bed, it would take a fucking army to get me to leave.

"Tell me to fuck you," I say when I can drag my lips from hers. She tries to lift and continue the kiss, but I need the words this time. I tighten my fingers in her hair to add a little bite. "Tell me to fuck you right now!"

"Please fuck me. Please, I need it so bad."

There is no second-guessing, no delay, or consideration. Who knows when I might be snatched away? Leaning down, I steal another hot kiss before ripping her pretty dress over her head. The bra follows after it landing somewhere on the other side of the room. I feel disgusted with myself for barely touching this perfection last time—for taunting her hot, little nipples with a knife when I should have worshiped them with my mouth and tongue.

But that's okay. I'll pay my dues by driving her fucking wild this time.

Her fingers fist my hair as I lower my head and suck the tip into my mouth. She groans, growing restless under me as I tug it gently. Never leaving off, I push, first one and then the other knee between her thighs and drop a little weight onto her to keep her still.

My T-shirt has gotten rucked up, and I can feel her hot, panty-covered pussy wedged against my abs.

"God, please!" She is tugging on my hair, but I'm not about the leave off this tit until it's good and sore from my attention. I swirl my tongue around the tight bud before sucking it into my mouth again. She groans, and her fingers clench over my hair.

I kiss every inch of exposed flesh from her throat to her belly button visible above the waist of her panties. And when she's a mess of need and begging, I finally edge them down and kiss what's exposed. I don't want to stop fucking kissing, but I need to get her panties off so I can get to my goal.

She half fights with me in her eagerness to be rid of her panties, ass wriggling and tits jiggling as she helps to get them off.

They land with a soft whoosh, but I pay them no heed. I'm too busy staring at Avery naked and ready for me. Her small hands tug impatiently at my T-shirt. I drag it over my head and toss it to the floor. Then I'm coaxing her legs open because I need a fucking taste, and I need her to fucking come.

This perfect, naked, and wet little pussy is all mine. "Mmnnn!" Her words are utter nonsense as I eat her out. The little twitching, gasping, and hair gripping tells me when I'm getting all the right spots. I want to get her off. I want to get her off hot and fast, and I want it more than my next breath.

I've never felt this desperation. This intense need for connection. The satisfaction that consumes me when she throws her head back and rides my face through her climax is experienced soul deep.

I wipe off my mouth on the back of my hand as she lays panting. I need to get inside her, and I need inside her now. I have a queue of absolutely filthy things I want to do to her. It's like I'm terrified this will be over, and she will be gone, and I will never see her again. But I also need to go slow because I didn't go slow last time.

All we've done so far is spit daggers, guilt, and rage at one another. There is no trust, but there needs to be trust.

Today I need to build her trust.

Her eyes pop open as I shift and push my pants down my thighs.

"Not my ass," she says like she's still thinking of me as a fucking savage.

I am a savage, but I can temper it, and I will. "I'm not gonna fuck your ass today," I say. "I make no allowances for tomorrow."

She gives me a look that says she's not sure if I'm joking.

"I'm joking, baby. I was so fucking angry last time. I didn't understand. I still don't, if I'm honest." I cup her face as I move to cage her body. "But I don't blame you anymore. And I don't hate you. You're not the monster I thought you were. Can you trust me? Can you let me show you that I was wrong?"

She nods. There are tears in her eyes as her hands lift to my cheeks. I feel them trembling as I lower my mouth over hers. She opens to the kiss and her tongue tangles with mine.

"So fucking sweet for an evil-minded god," I say against her lips.

Then I lift her knees up and slide inside her hot, clenching cunt.

CHAPTER SEVEN

Avery

Everything about this is so different from last time that there are no points to compare. The feeling of his fat cock sliding deep into me is both welcome and sublime. Nerves bloom to life as every glorious, thick inch glides oh-so-slowly inside. I could weep for the joy. Even when he bottoms out and his hips rest flush to mine, there is no pain, only bliss.

Knees spread wide, he braces over me—a dark, beautiful, deadly monster with an insanely built body.

He rocks his hips, and even this tiny movement fills my

heart and body with pleasure, made all the more intense because it is *him*. I fantasied about him, of course, in the early days when I was only writing a book. Later, when I began to meet him in the dreamscape of my sacred chamber, those fantasies changed. I still wanted him, but they were tempered by the visceral hatred he carried around like a shield.

I suffer so much guilt over what happened unwittingly by my design. I need this, whatever this is. I need to repent, and the handing over of my body and my life to him feels a worthy exchange.

"I need to hurt," I say.

His face shutters. "No."

"I need to be punished," I say.

He stills above me, buried deep, making everything clench up. "Still fucking no. Not this time, and not now."

I slap him hard across the face. "I need to be fucking punished."

He tries to grab my hands, but I'm determined, and I land more blows. I've never struck a person in my life, and I don't know what the hell is wrong with me. "You said you didn't want a fucking savage," he says, finally capturing my wrists and dropping enough weight onto me to keep me still.

I fight with him, and I don't care that all I'm doing is wearing myself out. "I want the savage. I don't even care where you put it so long as it's rough."

"Fuck," he mutters, and something in the tone takes the fight out of me.

I blink up at him in the soft, muted light. Why do I feel like I have said those words before? Why do I feel like I'm falling into something?

"I want to fall," I say. "I can feel myself slipping, and I want to fall. All the way. I feel so fucking guilty. I want to fucking forget."

"You have a filthy fucking mouth," he says, pinching my cheeks between his fingers and thumb. The pressure is a little achy, and it makes me clench up inside.

He groans and lowers his lips over mine. I strain and wriggle under him even as I open to the kiss. Catching his bottom lip between my teeth, I bite hard.

"Fuck!" His roar makes me a little scared, and I like being scared.

I *want* to be scared. There is blood on his lips, and I lick my own, tasting the coppery tang of the blood. "Try and kiss me, and I will bite you again."

"And you call me a fucking savage? What the fuck have I created?" He groans as I clench over his cock, growing restless when he refuses to move.

Is this the new book? Is this change in me part of his design? Are we already falling into the wormhole?

I think we are. I believe this is the beginning of my end.

He shifts suddenly, pulling out, and I whimper at the loss. My wrists are gathered together in one hand above my head. A wicked gleam lights his eyes as he crawls over me. I blink up at him as he closes his fingers securely around my throat. "I'm going to fuck my cock so deep down your throat, I'll be able to feel it under my hand."

I should be horrified.

But my pussy clenches, and I all but drool at the thought of tasting him.

His smirk is dark.

I open my mouth and push out my tongue.

"Fuck," he groans softly. His fingers leave my throat long enough to line his cock up with my mouth, and he sinks just the head inside. "You bite, and you won't like the consequence. Are we clear?"

I hum around the head, already lashing it with my tongue and sucking all the pre-cum up. I'm so hot and needy. There is a foreign pressure building up inside me. Everything is amplified, the harsh saw of his breathing, the musky scent of his cock, the taste of him in my mouth sets a tingling inside my pussy and all across my breasts.

I've come once, but I feel like I'm climbing toward another one, and he's barely touching me.

His domination is precisely what my battered, guilt-riddled soul needs.

My chest saws as his hand returns to my throat. His dark hair falls over his forehead, and his swirling eyes are almost black. He is impossibly monstrous as he towers over me, powerful, controlling. I need this. I need to be punished.

"Brace yourself," he says.

The first thrust strains my jaw, although I reason that it's not so deep.

The second makes me gag, and I think I might be sick.

"Breathe through your nose," he says, plunging straight back in.

The third one goes so deep it cuts off the air no matter how I breathe. Saliva pools in my mouth as he begins to shuttle in and out. I can't get enough air. I feel dizzy and faint. My spit is leaking everywhere, and my jaw and throat shift from ache toward pain.

"That feels so fucking good," he says as he fucks into my throat. "Tight, hot, clenching, I'm already fucking close."

Light fades. I'm sinking into darkness as the world turns to sparkles. He pulls almost out, and I heave hoarse breaths before he plunges again.

I squeeze my thighs together, groaning and gasping around his thick length. Between my legs, I'm wet and slippery.

"You were made for this, baby."

My body wants to struggle and fight for the next breath. But my mind is floating at peace, and the blackness welcomes me in.

The arrival of air shocks me from the bliss. I blink up through watery eyes at the dark angel staring down at me. His cock jerks as it hangs close to my lips while his fingers tighten around my throat until it aches so good. "Your pussy is about to get fucked so deep you won't walk straight for a week."

"Yes. Please! I want it."

He shifts. I'm flipped over onto my stomach, where I collapse in a heap. My hips are dragged up and back, and his cock breaches me. My pussy convulses around him. With Haden's alien cock inside me, I find deliverance from my guilt.

The hard, fast fucking takes me straight over the edge.

Deep inside, a hot flood of his seed bathes the entrance to my womb. That he doesn't stop drives home that he is an alien and not a man. The sting as his teeth sink into my throat is perfection.

I lose myself in the carnality of the night. I am wild and demanding. I sob and plead for more the moment he tries to allow me to rest. For the first time in my life, I feel the freedom to embrace my desires. Here in the arms of a man not of this world, I am finally home.

I don't want sleep to take me because I fear that Haden will be gone when I wake up. I am terrified of this ending and by the possibility of never seeing him again.

Maybe I should drag myself from the bed, open my laptop, and start writing again?

No, I never want to write again. This wreckage of my making has broken me in ways this fierce lover never could.

As my mind fights to pull of sleep, the words he had me write come back to me.

"She speaks the vows, binding herself to me for life. The heavy burden of her guilt will be assuaged through her deliverance to me for punishment and pleasure."

The words rock me and comfort me all at once. *Punished.* How I crave his brand of loving punishment.

I try so hard to stay awake, but as is inevitable, sleep drags me down.

CHAPTER EIGHT

Avery

"You're not supposed to see your betrothed on the morning of the ceremony," a male voice says somewhere in the room.

Betrothed?

I'm in bed, under a thick blanket. It's as cold as a tomb in the room where my nose peeks out of the covers. The rest of me is toasty warm . . . And pressed up against firm male flesh.

"Like I give a fuck," Haden says. "Why are you even in

here? What the fuck is the time?"

His hands tighten on me suddenly, and I emit a small squeak.

"Oh," Haden says, voice deepening to a growl that makes my chest flutter and my pussy clench. "Look what we have here." Teeth nip against my shoulder, and a big hand moves to cup my breast.

I shiver. But not from the cold.

I am here.

I am in *his* world.

In his bed.

About to say the vows that will bind me to him for the remainder of our lives.

"The wormhole?" I whisper.

"The wormhole," he agrees, a smile in his voice. I don't need to glance back to know his grin is showing his fangs.

The planet where he lives is all ice and snow. Resources are scarce, and they are at war with the people they share the planet with. The fortress he calls home is carved into a mountainside, high enough that the upper-reaches are sometimes lost in the clouds.

"They have started ringing the bells," the snooty voice continues. Layton, Haden's assistant, sounds exactly as I imagined he would. "But if you are otherwise indisposed, there is always next year."

Ignoring our visitor, I twist so I can look back at the male who holds me. There is a strange warmth in my chest as I come to terms with where I am and what this means. "Is this real?" I ask.

"What is real?" he counters.

I shake my head because I don't know anymore.

"My lord, the bells."

I bite my lip as a savage expression drops over Haden's face. I have seen that expression often, for it was often directed at me. All those visits to the sacred chamber have left a lasting impression upon my mind: so many meetings, over so many years where we have bickered. But we have also grown to know one another. Firstly, with suspicion and hate, but more lately, with understanding.

Instinctively, I know I shall never visit my sacred chamber again.

Just as I know I shall never write again.

Here, I am a minion and the subject of another god's whims.

Here, I do not conjure adventures, but I will live them for myself.

"Surely only a real place could come with such an annoying fucking assistant," Haden growls, turning his scowl to the man in question who is still lingering beside the bed.

I follow his line of sight. Layton, his assistant, is a slender male half Haden's size. His iridescent green skin is mostly covered by a neat black robe. He is both beautiful and alien. And unfazed by Haden's grouch.

All this feels both ordinary and natural.

How unexpected it is to be an integral part of this new, wondrous life?

Layton claps his hands, and a gaggle of green-skinned ladies, every bit as beautiful as Layton, pour into the room. They carry a dress.

My dress.

My mating ceremony dress.

For Haden has determined that my punishment will only be fulfilled by a lifetime of servitude to him.

And I want that.

With a huff, Haden rises from the bed, entirely naked, and stalks across the room. He pauses at the door as my helpers all but drag me from the bed. "I will return before you leave," Haden says, and there is something dark in his eyes that brings a flutter low in my belly. He does not like to be interrupted, but he wants me bound to him more.

So my preparations begin, for as Layton says, the bells are ringing, and soon they will stop, and the ceremony will start. I am cleansed and fussed over as they prepare me to be bound. My hair is coiled, and my body is covered in a rich, crimson gown. Where my culture lingers on the purity of the mate, here, my clothing represents the exchange of blood during sex for newly bonded couples.

As the bells stop ringing, the bedding chamber door opens, and Haden returns.

His swirling amber eyes darken as he drinks me in.

"Out!" he commands, and the sweet, bustling, green-skinned assistants flee the room in a flutter.

He approaches me with swift strides that set everything awakening in me. *"He only has to look at me, and I feel my body respond."*

I suck a deep breath as this fierce warrior grasps my beautifully coiled hair in his fist. "Bend over," he says.

I'm given no opportunity to do so when he thrusts me face-first over the table. My body tingles in anticipation, and my pussy clenches with need. "I'm going to fuck you," he says. Grasping the hem of my beautiful dress, he drags it up my legs and over my naked ass. "I want your pussy dripping with my cum while you are giving me your vows."

I groan as rough fingers pet my needy pussy. *"It doesn't matter how roughly he fucks me. I still come for him."*

The jiggle of his belt is unbearably loud. The feeling of his thick cock filling me a moment later, perfect in every way.

"We don't have a lot of time," he says, thrusting into me

with rough urgency, pounding my smaller body against the table as he takes his pleasure from me and gives equal pleasure back.

I beg him for more, for harder. For him to fill me up well so that I will feel where he has fucked me when I'm saying the vows.

And he does, and I come so hard my whole body shakes and spasms around his monstrous alien cock.

After, he is gentle. Fangs flashing, he smirks at what he has done.

He escorts me from the bedroom, along the fortress's stone corridors, and into the great chamber where the vows will be said. We are not alone in this. The vast vaulted chamber is full of other couples making their life pledge.

But I barely see the grandeur of the great stone room or the beautifully dressed citizens who surround us. I only have eyes for one person, and my obsession has come full circle upon me.

As the ceremony draws to a close, those committing are given leave to cement their joining with a kiss.

There is savagery in his swirling eyes as he looks upon me. I can feel his cum inside me, feel the soreness where he took me roughly. Leaning down, he cups my face in his strong hands. But he does not kiss me. Instead, he whispers in my ear, "Come for your master."

His lips cover mine as I splinter into a wild climax. He

holds me, swallowing my wild moans in a hot kiss.

I lean into him, grasping him, clutching for a lifeline in the storm. Trying to find ground and failing hopelessly.

When I finally recover my wits, I find my life-mate smirking.

He strokes a tender finger over my flushed cheeks. "Now," he says, smiling broad enough to flash fangs.

"I will take you back to my bedding chamber where your loving punishment will begin."

The End.

ABOUT THE AUTHOR

I love a happy ever after, although sometimes the journey to get there can be rough on my poor characters.

An unashamed fan of the alpha, the antihero, and the throwback in all his guises and wherever he may lurk.

I'm a new author, learning as I go and appreciate feedback of all kinds.

Drop me a message and let me know what you think.

Website: www.authorlvlane.com

Facebook Page: www.facebook.com/LVLaneAuthor/

Facebook group: www.facebook.com/groups/LVLane/

Goodreads: www.goodreads.com/LVLane

Amazon: www.amazon.com/author/lvlane

Printed in Great Britain
by Amazon